YOUNG EXPLORERS

THE SHADOW AND THE GOLDEN ROOM

Place SUCCESS BADGE here! Read page 73 to learn how to get it.

SOLVED

Written by J. I. Wagner. Illustrated by J. G. Ratti. Translated by T. Phua.

All rights reserved. Copyright 2021 by J. I. Wagner. Published by freshabooks. freshabooks is an imprint of: freshamedia GmbH, Robert-Bosch-Str. 32, 63303 Dreieich, Germany.

www.timmitobbson.com | www.freshabooks.com

ISBN 978-3-96326-701-7

Printed in the United States of America.

Hi. I'm Timmi.

I may not be the most confident boy. Or the most athletic. Or the best at anything. But I *am* quite curious. That seems to be good.

This is Lilli.

She can be stubborn. And sassy. But above all, she is the bravest and most loyal person I know. She'd do anything to help you.

This is Marvin.

He loves animals. Whenever he gets excited, he bobs up and down on the spot. And he claps. It looks silly, but he doesn't care.

The Young Explorers

This is our own little club. We want to help others and train to one day get accepted as students at Backalley One.

Pssst. Here is a secret mission. The seven items to the right can each be found on the following pages! Search for them and note the page number you found them on. Then go to timmitobbson.com and find the secret area. Enter the page numbers to pass the security check. A surprise awaits you!

Backalley One

A secret club for great adventurers and detectives who solve mysteries no one else can. We recently found its hidden location.

This is Boris.

Boris is the head of Backalley One. We've only met him once. He accepted us as early apprentices and told us we would hear from him once we were ready. We are still waiting.

This is Tom.

Unbelievable. My older brother is a student at Backalley One! He works with Boris. How could I not have noticed?

This is the story of how we got to help Backalley One for the first time ever.

Find:

Found on page:

THE SHADOW AND THE GOLDEN ROOM

FACTS
FOR EXPLORERS

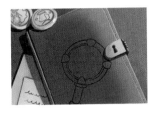

HANDBOOK
FOR EXPLORERS

HIDDEN IN PLAIN SIGHT

"Finally," said Timmi. "We thought something had happened to you."

"No, I'm fine," said Tom. "But they're freaking out over at Backalley."

"What's going on?" asked Marvin.

"And what are you doing with all those newspapers?" I asked.

Tom saw our eager faces and smiled.

"Okay," he said. "I need your help."

"A mission from Backalley One!" cried Marvin.

"Whatever it is, we're in," said Lilli.

Buckalley believes The Shadow will strike tonight," whispered Tom.

"The Shadow?" I asked.

"He's a master villain responsible for lots of big, unsolved crimes," Tom went on. "No-one knows what he looks like."

We all listened intently.

He has only ever been seen after dark.
Legend has it he can vanish into the
night shadows without a trace," Tom said.

"But that's nonsense," said Lilli.

"One moment he's there," said Tom
and snapped his fingers. "The next, he's
gone."

"We might be able to catch him tonight," said Tom. "Seems he's putting the Golden Room up for sale." Tom stared at us expectantly. "Haven't you heard of it?" he asked.

We shook our heads.

"It's a room with walls made of gold. Incredibly valuable," he said, showing us a picture. "The room was built hundreds of years ago. Then it was supposedly destroyed. But that's just a myth. The Shadow has gotten hold of it. He's going to sell it tonight."

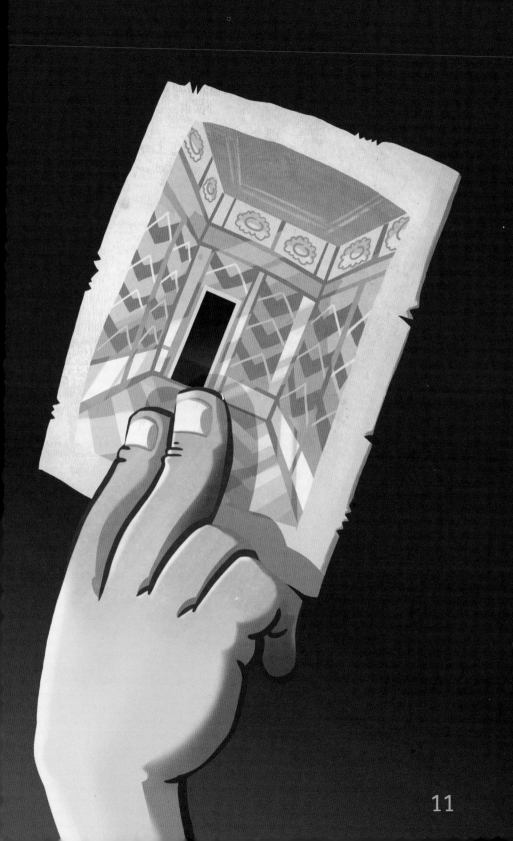

According to our informant, the time and location of the sale are hidden in a newspaper," said Tom, pointing to the pile next to him. "But we don't know which one."

"Oh," sighed Lilli. "We have to search that whole pile? What are we looking for?"

"A secret message consisting of three parts. A photo of lightning, one of fire, and a list of city landmarks. All in the same newspaper," said Tom, slapping a stack of them into Lilli's lap.

Time crept by. We searched paper after paper, but no luck. We were getting tired.

"I've got it!" yelled Tom suddenly.

"Lightning, fire and the landmarks. They're all here!"

He quickly tore the pictures from his newspaper and lay them out.

"It says 9H by the lightning," he mused. "Coordinates to go with the table. 9H stands for The Statue of the Inventor. That must be where it's going down." "And by the fire it says when it's happening," I replied. "But that's only twenty minutes from now!"

"I have to let Backalley know. They'll need all hands on deck," said Tom. "But you kids are done for tonight. Sorry. Thanks again." We protested loudly, but he just stormed out of the room.

"Great," I said, and for a few minutes, we all lay on the floor staring at the ceiling in disappointment. In the end, my gaze wandered back to the pieces of newspaper. Something wasn't right.

"Oh no," I said. "Tom made a mistake. They're meeting at a totally different place."

The solution to each puzzle is revealed at the beginning of the following chapter.
You can find hints at the back of this book.

What mistake did Tom make?

THE STAKEOUT

Tom had been looking at the picture of lightning upside down. The correct coordinates were H6. The meeting place was the old cinema! Tom had drummed it into us never to discuss sensitive information over the phone, so we jumped on our bikes and pedaled as fast as we could over to Backalley One.

When we arrived, Boris opened the door holding a candle.

"Good evening Boris, sir," I said.

"We urgently need to talk to you."

"Then come in, quick," he said and stepped aside.

Once inside, we told Boris about Tom's mistake.

"They've all left already," said Boris. "I have no choice but to ask for your help."

"No problem," said Lilli.

"Head straight off on your bikes, along our network of hidden alleys. Follow the arrows labelled BTWO till you come to a blue door. I'll give you the key. Sneak up to the second floor where you'll find an empty room. You'll be able to stake out the old cinema from there."

something off a bookshelf as he passed.
"You're going to need this." He threw a
helmet with an antenna to Marvin and a
slimy ball to Lilli.

"What on earth is *this*?" she asked.

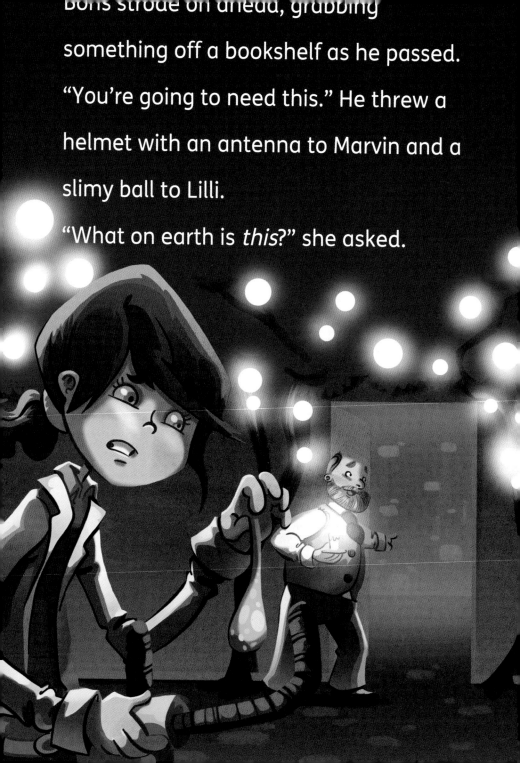

"That's Slimy. It's a bug," said Boris when we reached the inner courtyard leading to the hidden alleys. "It'll stick to anything. A house wall for example. It transmits any sounds it picks up through to Marvin's helmet. You can use it to eavesdrop on the gangsters. Off you go now. I'll send Tom and the others along as soon as I can."

The moon cast a spooky glow over the hidden alleyways, but our bike lights helped. It was great fun speeding down the narrow paths. We soon found the blue door and moments later entered the room whose windows offered a view of the opposite side of the street.

'There's the old cinema," whispered Lilli.

'Look," I said. "Those must be the gangsters."

'Is that The Shadow on the left behind that tall table?" asked Marvin.

'I bet it is," I said. "I bet he's telling them the rules of the sale."

Now the group began to move. They left the room, and moments later one gangster after the other exited the cinema downstairs. They each got into separate cars and drove off.

"You can't see the number plates," I whispered. "It's too dark down there."

"We can't let them get away," said Marvin.

"Wait," said Lilli. "I think the man with the yellow umbrella is The Shadow. I'm sure it was him standing at the table and speaking to the others."

How could Lilli tell?

THE CHASE IS ON

"The gloves and the walking stick," whispered Lilli. "They belong to the man who was behind that tall table. It must be The Shadow."

"He's getting in," I said. "They're going to drive off."

"We have to get our bikes," yelled Marvin. "After them!"

"Hang on," said Lilli, sliding the window open. "Boris didn't give us this disgusting ball for nothing."

With that, she threw Slimy at the car.

It landed on the roof with a gentle plop!

The passengers didn't seem to notice.

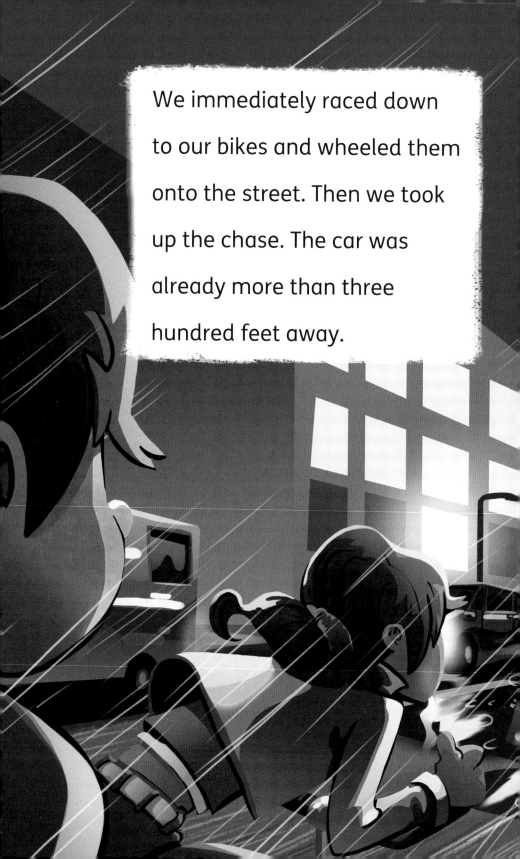

We immediately raced down to our bikes and wheeled them onto the street. Then we took up the chase. The car was already more than three hundred feet away.

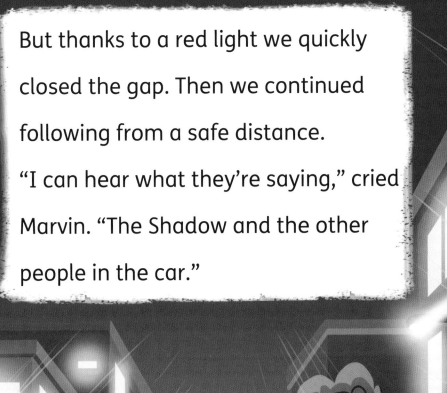

But thanks to a red light we quickly closed the gap. Then we continued following from a safe distance.

"I can hear what they're saying," cried Marvin. "The Shadow and the other people in the car."

"What? Tell us!" I yelled.

"They're going to the Golden Room. The buyers want to see it before they pay."

A few minutes later, we were riding through Chinatown. In a side street, the car we were tailing stopped. The Shadow and the other four passengers got out.

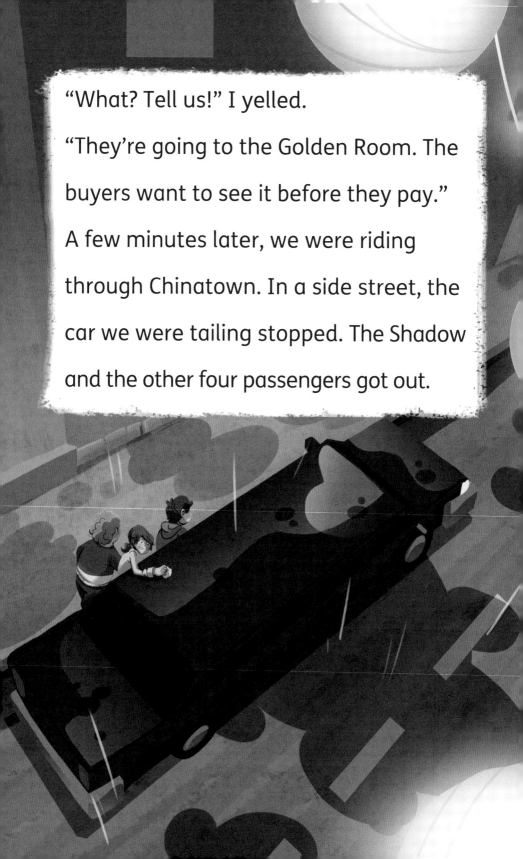

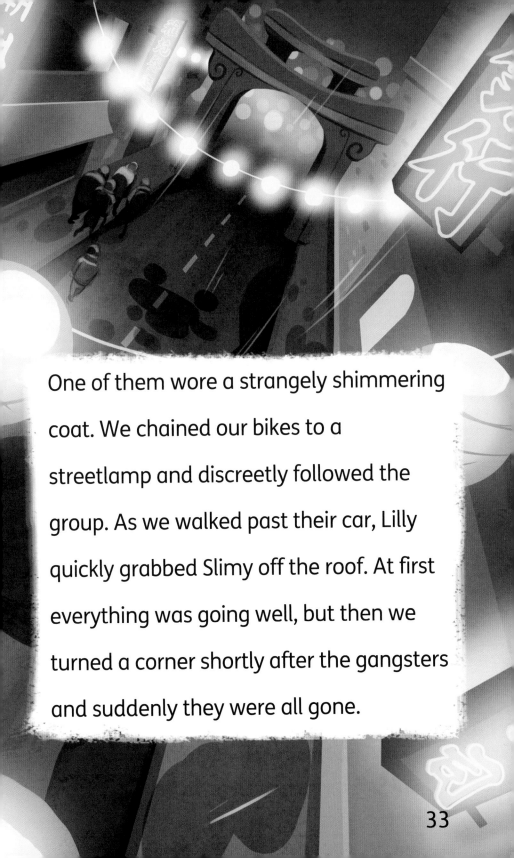

One of them wore a strangely shimmering coat. We chained our bikes to a streetlamp and discreetly followed the group. As we walked past their car, Lilly quickly grabbed Slimy off the roof. At first everything was going well, but then we turned a corner shortly after the gangsters and suddenly they were all gone.

"They vanished!" said Marvin, eyes wide. "Just like Tom said."

"Nonsense," said Lilli. "But we need a spot with a better view."

She promptly raced up the steps of some scaffolding in front of a building.

"Come on," she called.

"Same old Lilli," I said.

"Yep, same old Lilli," Marvin replied.

We dashed after her. Arriving at the top, Lilli pointed across the street. "Look! I think three of the people in front of the toy store are lookouts in disguise. They have something unusual in common."

What is it they have in common?

THE GOLDEN ROOM

"They're all wearing the same weird glasses," I said.

"Exactly. I read an article in one of Tom's papers tonight about glasses like those," said Lilli. "They're spy glasses with state-of-the-art technology. They even have a built-in telescopic lens."

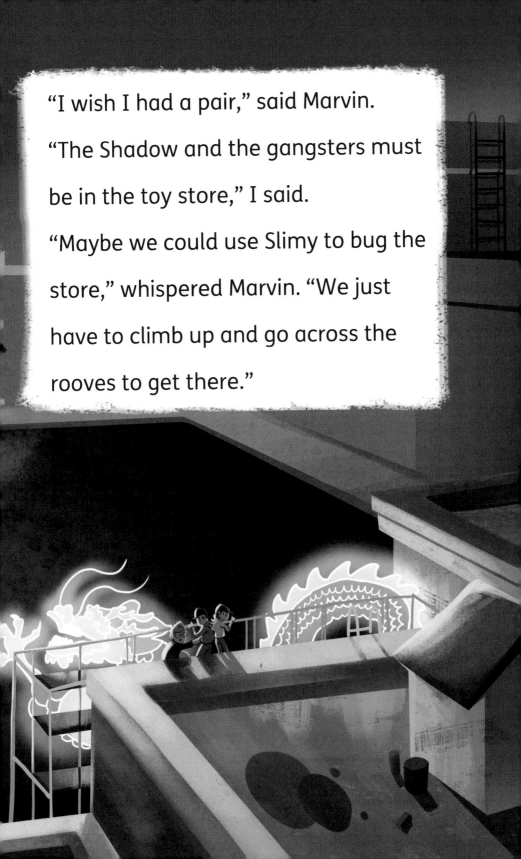

"I wish I had a pair," said Marvin.

"The Shadow and the gangsters must be in the toy store," I said.

"Maybe we could use Slimy to bug the store," whispered Marvin. "We just have to climb up and go across the rooves to get there."

We hurried across the rooftops, ducking behind chimneys to avoid being seen by the lookouts with the special glasses. Finally we made it to the toy store.

On its roof was a window that allowed us to peek inside.

"Those are the gangsters who want to buy the Golden Room," whispered Marvin.

"But it looks like they're checking out toys," whispered Lilli.

"It's not the toys they're looking at," I said. "Don't you see the walls? They're golden!"

"Here comes our guy," said Marvin.

Directly below us, The Shadow appeared.

He put a hand to his ear and stopped still.

"Looks like he's listening to someone,"
I whispered.

Suddenly he turned, pointed at us, and
yelled something. We drew back in fright.

Just then the light went out in the store,

only to flicker back on an instant later.

"He's gone!" yelled Marvin. "Disappeared!"

"He must have escaped through the front

door," I said. "Or a window."

"No, he used that trapdoor," said Lilli.

 What made Lilli think so?

THE STORE THAT WASN'T

"The handle of the trapdoor," Lilli said. "It was facing the other way before. He must have escaped through there."

"We should get out of here too," said Marvin and jumped up.

But I was frozen to the spot.

I had just caught a glimpse of someone I thought I recognized. It was the man with the strangely shimmering coat who had gotten out of The Shadow's car earlier.

"I think that's one of the Nine Twins," I said. "They're working for The Shadow!"

Could that be?

At first, I didn't get what happened next. All the gangsters had left the store in a hurry. Suddenly the sign over the toy store was pulled down like a garage door. The next moment, the roof moved beneath our feet! Lilli and Marvin lost their balance and fell onto their bottoms in surprise. The whole toy store was now in motion.

"It's a truck," I finally realized.

With a lurch and a rumble, the truck

pulled into the night traffic.

"No way!" I yelled.

Quick-thinking as ever, Lilli chucked

Slimy onto the cab of the truck.

"Marvin!" she yelled.

He immediately put the receiver helmet on. "They've somehow set all the traffic lights to green," yelled Marvin. "The truck has a clear path all the way to its destination. It's going to the harbor."

"That means we can't jump off," I said.

"We have to get down," I yelled. "Come
on. In there for a start."

We opened the window in the roof and
dropped inside. Marvin continued to
listen to everything the driver said while
Lilli and I searched for a way out. Lilli
opened the secret trapdoor.

"We can forget that," she said. "It leads straight onto the street."

I stumbled, struggling to stay on my feet, and suddenly noticed something strange. The Golden Room seemed to be sliding back and forth. *What's going on here?*

I wanted to see how the Golden Room was attached to the truck. To find out, I grabbed the cord attached to the cargo door and yanked it up.

"Don't open it!" Lilli yelled, but her warning came too late. The cargo door had already slid upwards.

"There are ropes behind the walls," I cried. "They're holding the room on."

Having confirmed my suspicion, I wanted to close the cargo door again. I reached for the cord to pull it back down.

"Don't touch that handle!" yelled Lilli.

 What was Lilli worried about?

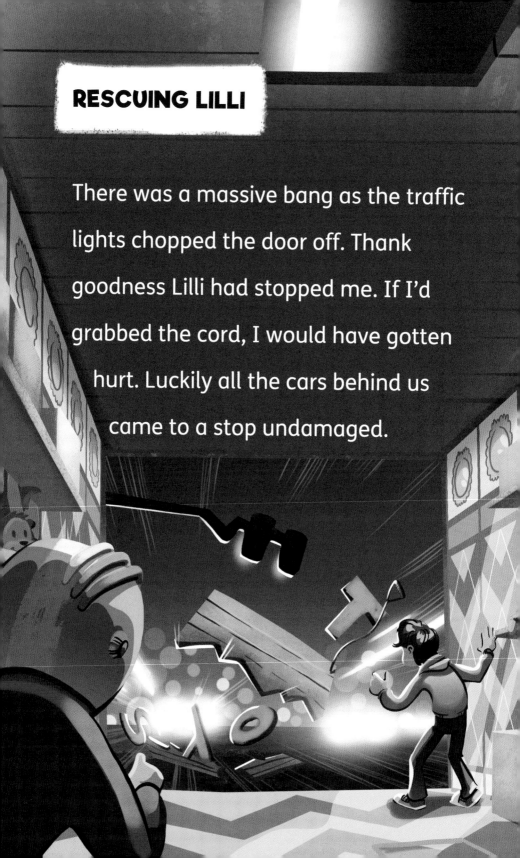

RESCUING LILLI

There was a massive bang as the traffic lights chopped the door off. Thank goodness Lilli had stopped me. If I'd grabbed the cord, I would have gotten hurt. Luckily all the cars behind us came to a stop undamaged.

I clung to the wall in shock.

"Somehow we have to get out of here," yelled Marvin. "The guy from the Nine Twins gang is driving. He must be one of the masterminds behind this. He's going to leave the truck at the harbor and disappear into the crowd so no-one can link him to all this."

"We can't let him see us," I said. "But we also can't jump off at this speed."

"No, jumping off isn't an option," said Lilli. "But maybe there's something else we can do." Lilli had found a door connecting the Golden Room to the main cargo area of the truck.

"What are you doing?" I asked.

"Hold on tight," she yelled.

Now I saw that Lilli was clutching a large lever. *That lever doesn't release the ropes holding the Golden Room on the truck, does it?*

"No Lilli, wait!" I yelled.

But she had no intention of waiting.

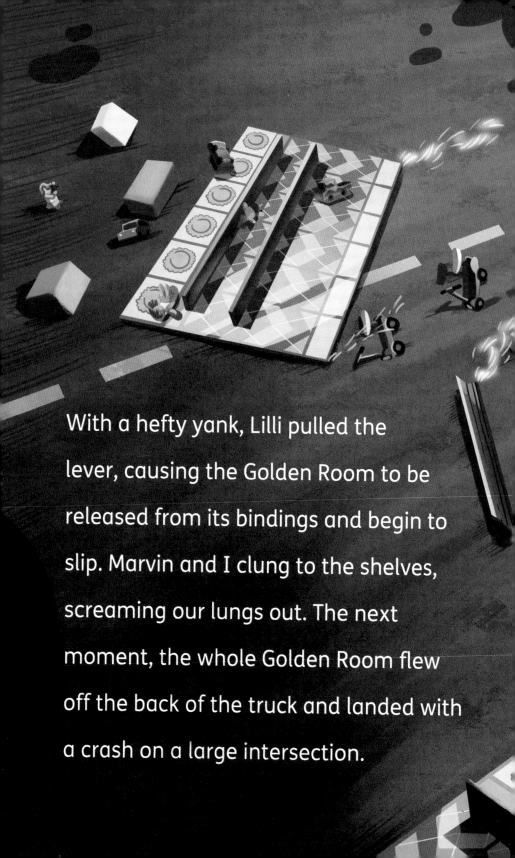

With a hefty yank, Lilli pulled the lever, causing the Golden Room to be released from its bindings and begin to slip. Marvin and I clung to the shelves, screaming our lungs out. The next moment, the whole Golden Room flew off the back of the truck and landed with a crash on a large intersection.

Plastic shattered and chunks of wall flew everywhere. It seemed to be raining gold and colored confetti. The floor, with us on top, slid several feet farther across the pavement before suddenly coming to a stop. An eerie silence followed.

"Where's Lilli?" I asked.

Marvin and I watched the truck drive off.

Lilli was still standing in the back of it.

"Oh no!" said Marvin. "We've got to go

after her."

"It's downhill from here all the way to the

harbor," I said. "Let's take the scooters!"

Without thinking it through much, we each grabbed one of the scooters lying nearby and headed off. The truck was still faster than us, but we knew where it was going. By the time we lost sight of it, we didn't have far to go.

A few minutes later, we reached a cliff
at the edge of the city. Its great lake
shimmered in the moonlight. From here,
the street wound its way downhill to the
harbor.

"Lilli?" Marvin suddenly yelled and
grabbed his helmet.

I wanted to listen too, so I pressed my ear onto the outside.

"Yeah, I'm okay," came the crackly reply. I felt like a huge weight had been lifted off my shoulders. Marvin and I cheered. Once we had calmed down, we asked Lilli what had happened.

"The Twin ran away. He probably went into one of the bars here. But I don't know which one. I don't want to lose him."

"Try to concentrate," I said. "What did you see and hear?"

"I heard him running over gravel, then he opened the door to a bar. I couldn't see which one. But when he did, light streamed out from inside and the music got louder," said Lilli. "Hang on, I think I know where he went now."

Which bar did the Twin enter?

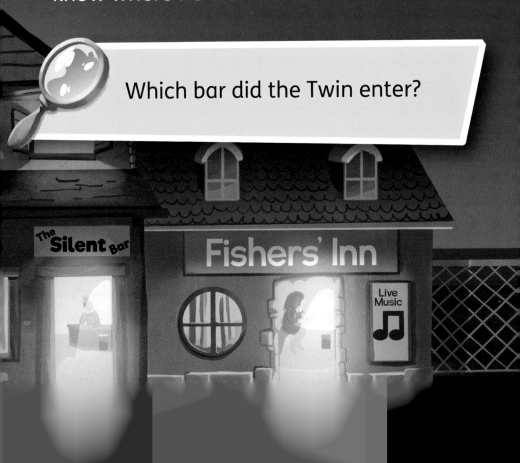

The Silent Bar

Fishers' Inn

Live Music

OBSERVATION IS KEY

Only the door of the bar on the left wasn't made of glass, which meant that more light streamed out once it was opened. That had to be where he was. We met Lilli in the little alley beside the bar.

"He's in there," she said, peeking through a window. "The waiter just brought soup."

"Hey, the keys to the truck are on the table," said Marvin. "They could prove he was the driver."

"Time to call the police," I said. "There's a payphone here. Anyone got a coin?"

"You can call emergency services without one," said Marvin.

When a police officer arrived, we pointed out the Twin to him through the side window. The truck keys were still next to his soup. We followed the officer inside, but when we arrived at the gangster's table they were gone! The policeman ordered the crook to get up.

He then frisked him, but didn't find anything.

"I'm innocent," said the Twin. "There were no keys here."

"He hid them," I said. "And I think I know where, too."

Where did the Twin hide his keys?

THE CAKE AND THE PROMISE

"The soup comes farther up the inside of the bowl now," I said and fished the keys out with a spoon.

Marvin clapped his hands and bobbed up and down.

"You're under arrest," said the policeman and put handcuffs on the gangster.

"Are you the kids who got my brother thrown in jail?" he asked.

We weren't about to admit to that, so we kept quiet and the Twin glared angrily at us as he was led away.

"I could go for a piece of cake right now," said Lilli.

"You know where I saw cake just before?" asked Marvin excitedly.

A half hour later, we were sitting in the living room at Backalley One. Tom had joined us, and we were eating cake when Boris stormed in. He seemed in a hurry. "We're still trying to find The Shadow," he said. "But congratulations, kids. You just have to promise me one thing. Next time don't take up the chase on your own. Wait for backup. Promise me that!"

"They can't speak with their mouths full, Boris, that would be rude," said Tom, giving us a wink.

We all nodded, then shoved extra big pieces of cake in our mouths, shrugging and trying to look innocent. Boris sighed, shook his head, and hurried back out of the room.

"What am I going to do with them?" we heard him muttering as he walked away.

THE END
(FOR NOW)

FACTS FOR EXPLORER

The students at Backalley One strive to solve mysteries, ancient and modern. To be successful, they need to know a lot. Here is a collection of fascinating facts taught at Backalley One that relate to this book's adventure.

Pssst. Get this book's Success Badge!

Collect all the letters displayed in the emblems on the following pages. Rearrange the letters to form two words. Then enter the words in the "Badges" section on timmitobbson.com to download your Success Badge. Print it out and paste it in its place on the first page to show you solved every mystery and read all the facts and tips for young explorers!

Even though he doesn't have any change on him, Timmi is able to call the police from a payphone. In most countries you can call emergency services from any telephone free of charge. Usually those numbers are only three digits long so that they're easy to remember.

In Europe and some Asian countries for example, they use the number 112, and in America it is 911. The first emergency telephone number in the world was used in London, England, in 1937. It was the number 999.

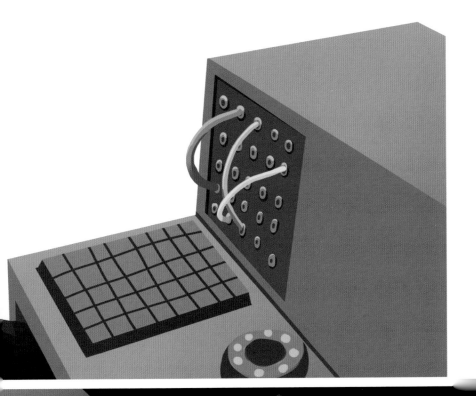

The meeting place for the sale of the Golden Room was announced by putting a secret message in a newspaper.

People have been putting encoded messages like that in newspapers for over two hundred years. They're published in small advertisements or hidden in articles. Criminals have used them to make their demands known to the police, and secret services have used them to give their spies orders from afar.

The Young Explorers watch the gangsters' secret meeting from an empty apartment. The police, too, often rent rooms to covertly observe suspects from. Usually teams of at least two officers are on duty.

That way, one can watch the target while the other documents the observations. In around half an hour they switch. The team should be replaced by another team after a few hours so no-one gets too tired.

Timmi, Marvin and Lilli pursue the gang by foot, by bike and even on scooters. But you should never pursue a suspect yourself! It can get dangerous fast. That's the kind of thing you need to leave to the police.

If the police want to discreetly follow a suspect, plain-clothes officers are used. Then they don't look like police officers; they look like perfectly ordinary citizens. Ideally the officers work in a team. Then they can regularly switch out the person in pursuit so the suspect doesn't notice one particular person.

The Golden Room doesn't really exist, but the "Amber Room" does. It was built around 1705 in Germany and was so luxurious that it was considered the "Eighth Wonder of the World". It was taken down during World War Two

and stored in crates to protect it from bombs. But it has never been seen since. Treasure hunters are still looking for it to this day. Incidentally, amber is made of fossilized tree resin. Pieces can be found on certain beaches after powerful storms. Sometimes small animals are preserved inside it.

Young apprentices get the classified Backalley One Handbook. Now *you* can apply its secrets and become a Young Explorer!

84

Some of the bad guys wore spy glasses with telescopic lenses and a rear-view mirror function. You can put a secret mirror into your glasses too. You'll be able to see what's going on behind you without anyone noticing.

You'll need a plastic mirror sheet, which you can find at a craft store, and a pair of glasses you're allowed to glue something to. Cut a piece of the mirror sheet to size and glue it inside the glasses (see illustration). The piece should be fitted to lie flat, not curved. Now you're all set!

Timmi noticed a small change that told him where the Twin had hidden his keys. Observation skills like this are valuable for all detectives. You can easily practice with a friend. Place five or more objects on a table. Now one of you

carefully memorizes how it is all laid out. Then they look away, while the other person changes something. Can they spot the difference? In the secret area of the Young Explorers Series on www.timmitobbson.com you'll also find "Spot the Difference" games to use in your detective training.

Slimy uses radio waves to transmit sounds to Marvin's helmet, but there is a simpler way. You can make your own cup phone using two plastic cups and a string. Poke a hole in the bottom of the cups.

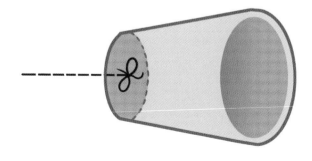

Then thread one end of the string through each hole and tie nice big knots in them, or tie them to little pieces of wood or paper clips. Then pull the string between the cups tight. Don't let it touch anything else. Now when someone speaks into one of the cups, you'll be able to hear it through the other.

The "Golden Room" is very valuable. Did you know that gold can be found in nature? You can search for it in areas known for gold deposits. Gold is usually found in or around rivers.

Equipped with a gold pan, you can pan for small pieces of gold on a river's gravel bar. Give it a try. But first check whether panning for gold is allowed in that spot and whether it will be okay for you to keep your find.

The newspaper picture Tom had up the wrong way showed a lightning bolt. Lightning can be very dangerous, especially when you're outdoors. As an adventurer, you need to know how to protect yourself.

Do you think Timmi picked a good spot?

You'll be safest in a house with a lightning rod or in a car. If neither are available, you should find the lowest spot in the area, but avoid open spaces where you would be the highest point. Make yourself small by crouching, don't lie down. Don't go near trees or water. Keep your distance from other people.

Pssst. Here are some hints!

page 17 Take a close look at the image showing the lightning. Does it look right to you? Tom read the coordinates as 9H. But really it is ... ?

page 27 Lilli believed the person with the yellow umbrella was the same one as they saw behind the table. Compare the people in the pictures. What do both have in common?

page 35 In the first chapter, Lilli saw a rather uncommon wearable item. Three people in front of the toy store seem to be using that same gadget.

page 40 Take a look at the trapdoor in the floor. Do you see something unusual? A change in the before and after image?

page 51 Lilli did not want Timmi to open the cargo door in the first place. Now that Timmi is reaching for the cord connected to the cargo door to pull it back down, she tells him to stop. What could happen to the cargo door and the cord connected to it? Examine the surroundings.

page 63 It seems music is played in at least two buildings and each has gravel in front. So Lilli's conclusion must have something to do with light.

page 67 Take a look at every item on the table. One has changed.